PEDRO

PIRATE PEDRO

by Fran Manushkin

illustrated by
Tammie Lyon

raintree
a Capstone company — publishers for children

Raintree is an imprint of Capstone Global Library Limited, a company incorporated
in England and Wales having its registered office at 264 Banbury Road, Oxford,
OX2 7DY – Registered company number: 6695582

www.raintree.co.uk
myorders@raintree.co.uk

Designed by Aruna Rangarajan and Tracy McCabe
Original illustrations © Capstone Global Library Limited 2020
Originated by Capstone Global Library Ltd
Printed and bound in India.

978 1 4747 8961 5 (paperback)

British Library Cataloguing in Publication Data
A full catalogue record for this book is available from the British Library.

Acknowledgements
We would like to thank the following for permission to reproduce design elements:
Shutterstock.

Contents

Chapter 1
Pirate Day

"Ahoy there! Wake up!"

said Pedro's dad. "It's Pirate

Day at school."

Pedro got up fast.

He ate his pirate pancakes

and put on his pirate hat.

"Goodbye," Pedro said.

"See you later, landlubbers!"

"Take me along!" said Paco.

"You are too little," said Pedro.

Peppy, Pedro's puppy, tried to come too.

"No!" said Pedro. "Puppies can't be pirates."

At school, Miss Winkle
said, "Hello, crew! Are you
ready to be pirates?"

"Arrr!" yelled Pedro and
Katie and JoJo.

"Can you unscramble

these pirate words?" asked

Miss Winkle.

"*Glaf* is flag!" said

Pedro. "And *words* is sword!"

"Right-o!" said Miss

Winkle.

Later on, Pedro made a
pirate flag.

"It's called a Jolly
Roger," said Katie. "They
named it after a happy
man called Roger."

JoJo told the class a story
about a girl pirate.

"Her name was Mary
Read," said JoJo. "She was
fierce!"

After school, Pedro said,

"Let's be pirates at my house."

"Arrr!" yelled Katie. "I'll be

the captain. I'm fierce – just

like Mary Read!"

"No way!" said Pedro.

"Being captain is my job."

Chapter 2
Pirates at Pedro's

Pedro's tree house was their

ship. He proudly put up the

Jolly Roger.

"I want to be a pirate too!" yelled Paco. He put on an eye patch and began running around.

"Watch out!" warned JoJo. "You are walking the plank!"

JoJo grabbed Paco before

he fell overboard!

"I think fast," JoJo bragged.

"That's why I should be the

captain."

"No! I should be captain,"
said Katie. "I have sharper
eyes. I can see a crow sitting
on our crow's nest."

"But I am strong," said

Pedro. "And brave! See my

sword? I can win any fight!"

Chapter 3

Who will be captain?

Suddenly, it began to rain.

"Don't worry," said Pedro.

"My ship is strong! It will keep

us dry through any storm."

Below the ship, Peppy was
rolling in the mud.

Oops! Pedro dropped his
sword in the puddle.

Peppy picked it up to fetch
it. He was a good fetcher.

"No!" yelled Pedro. "It is
not a stick. Don't bring it back
to me."

Did Peppy listen? No! He climbed the ladder and shook mud all over the pirates!

"Shiver me timbers!" shouted

Pedro. "It's fun getting wet!"

"Yes, it is!" yelled Katie,

laughing.

"Yes!" said JoJo. "We are jolly

pirates."

"We would
all be jolly
captains," said
Pedro. "Maybe
we should take
turns."

"I thought
that too," said
Katie.

"So did I!"
said JoJo.

Soon it was time for a snack of hot dogs and pirate pudding.

All the pirates agreed: it was very tasty!

About the author

Fran Manushkin is the author of many popular picture books, including *Happy in Our Skin*; *Baby, Come Out!*; *Latkes and Applesauce: A Hanukkah Story*; *The Tushy Book*; *Big Girl Panties*; and *Big Boy Underpants*. Fran writes on her beloved Mac computer in New York, USA, without the help of her two naughty cats, Chaim and Goldy.

About the illustrator

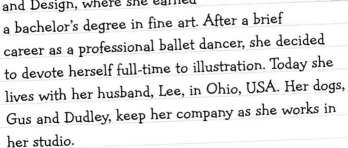

Tammie Lyon began her love of drawing at a young age while sitting at the kitchen table with her dad. She continued her love of art and eventually attended the Columbus College of Art and Design, where she earned a bachelor's degree in fine art. After a brief career as a professional ballet dancer, she decided to devote herself full-time to illustration. Today she lives with her husband, Lee, in Ohio, USA. Her dogs, Gus and Dudley, keep her company as she works in her studio.

Glossary

crow's nest small platform used for a lookout, found on top of the mast of a sailing ship

fierce daring and dangerous

landlubbers people who live on the land and know little or nothing about the sea

overboard over the side of a boat and into the water

walking the plank forced to walk along a board sticking out over the side of the ship and fall into the sea

Let's talk

1. Pedro and his friends celebrate Pirate Day at school. What activities do they do? If you could celebrate something at school, what would it be? What kind of activities would you do?

2. Pedro talks like a pirate several times in the story. What are some of the words or phrases he uses? Try talking like a pirate yourself.

3. Pedro thinks that a good captain is strong and brave. What else makes a good captain?

Let's write

1. Pedro is prepared for Pirate Day at school. Write about how you would prepare for Pirate Day. What would you wear?

2. Pedro and his friends decide to take turns being captain. Write about a time you and your friends took turns.

3. Pedro and his friends are jolly pirates and decide to be jolly captains. Look up the word 'jolly' and copy the definition. Then write any other words that mean the same thing.

✕ Why did the pirate buy the
eye patch?
He didn't have enough money
for an eye-pad.

✕ Why did it take the pirate so long
to learn the alphabet?
He spent years at C.

✕ When is the best time for a pirate
to buy their ship?
When it's on sail.

✕ Why can't pirates
play cards?
They are sitting
on the deck.

🦴 What is a pirate's
favourite animal?
an arrrrdvark

🦴 Why are pirates such good singers?
Because they can hit the high Cs!

🦴 What are pirates afraid of?
the darrrrk

🦴 What is a pirate's
least favourite
vegetable?
a leek

THE FUN DOESN'T STOP HERE!

Discover more stories and characters at

www.raintree.co.uk